EVIL JOURNEY

A screenplay

BY

OCHEI INNOCENT

MOVEMENT ONE

INT. MODERATELY FURNISHED APARTMENT. - DAY

THREE CHIEFS ARE SEATED.

CAST:

MRS. PHILLIPS

PHILLIPS

THREE CHIEFS

OLD WOMAN.

MRS. PHILLIPS

I advise that you leave please.

CHIEF JAMES

Shut up you this talkative woman!

CHIEF KOKO

How dare you?

CHIEF DIDI

We traveled a thousand kilometers to see our brother and you say we should leave when he is in this house?

MRS. PHILLIPS

He cannot hold a meeting this morning!

CHIEF KOKO

Why? Does he have a boil in his mouth?

MRS. PHILLIPS

He has a flight to catch in Abuja.

MRS. PHILLIPS

He does not need to tell me because I know he cannot see anyone now.

[Phillips comes in.]

PHILLIPS

Its okay Honey: I will see them.

MRS, PHILLIPS

No, you will not or you miss your flight.

PHILLIPS

Then, let me miss the flight.

[Mrs. Phillips leaves, banging the door]

CHIEF JAMES

This woman must be the reason why you have not been responding to our calls!

CHIEF KOKO

Exactly!

PHILLIPS

I have never failed to respond to you.

CHIEF DIDI

Not in recent times.

PHILLIPS

I am now managing myself.

CHIEF JAMES

Meaning what?

PHILLIPS

I am no longer a public servant.

CHIEF JAMES

Did you consult us before resigning?

PHILLIPS

I knew you would never accept it.

CHIEF KOKO

Look, we are not here for arguments.

PHILLIPS

Why are you here?

CHIEF JAMES

We are building a new town hall.

PHILLIPS

What is wrong with the old one?

CHIEF JAMES

All neighboring towns have big halls.

PHILLIPS

So?

CHIEF JAMES

We shortlisted ten of you to give us the money and others have paid except you.

PHILLIPS

I am just hearing of it.

CHIEF JAMES

Go inside and give us the money.

PHILLIPS

You will hear from me next week.

CHIEF KOKO

We need fuel money to go back.

[Phillips gives Koko who counts it.]

Ten thousand naira?

CHIEF DIDI

What?

CHIEF JAMES

Are you insulting us?

[Phillips adds another five thousand.]

CHIEF JAMES

Now you are talking!

[They laugh, shake hands and leave. An old woman comes in.]

OLD WOMAN

Why are you looking at me strangely?

PHILLIPS

Have we met before Ma?

OLD WOMAN

So what they said is true?

PHILLIPS

What is that?

OLD WOMAN

They said that you are very stingy and always pretend not to know people so that you cannot give a dime to them.

PHILLIPS

So they sent you to rebuke me for that?

OLD WOMAN

I came to see for myself.

PHILLIPS

Then go and tell them that I am stingy.

OLD WOMAN

How can I tell what I have not seen?

PHILLIPS

What else do you need to see?

OLD WOMAN

I have not eaten since yesterday.

PHILIPS

[Phillips hands her some money.]

OLD WOMAN

I now have full story to tell them.

PHILLIPS

What do you have to say to tell?

OLD WOMAN

That it is true that you go to Abuja, collect money with water tanks only to come and give us some with tablespoon!

[Phillips gently locks her out.]

MOVEMENT TWO

EXT. FRONT OF PHILLIPS' HOME. - DAY

CAST:

MRS. PHILLIPS

PHILLIPS.

MRS. PHILLIPS

So you are bent on this night journey?

PHILLIPS

That is the only option I have.

MRS. PHILLIPS

How can certain death be only option?

PHILLIPS

Others safely go and come same way!

MRS. PHILLIPS

Remember I told you before, how I dreamt that you died on this trip?

PHILLIPS

And I told you it is just a dream.

MRS. PHILLIPS

Why do you deceive yourself?

PHILLIPS

Stop giving yourself reasons to worry.

MRS. PHILLIPS

You know that my dreams never fail!

PHILLIPS

You fear night trips too much.

MRS. PHILLIPS

Please take the flight in the morning?

PHILLIPS

You want to hear the truth?

MRS. PHILLIPS

Which truth?

PHILLIPS

Instead of taking the flight I decided to donate the difference to all those asking me for money.

MRS. PHILLIPS

Do you hear yourself?

PHILLIPS

Relax: I will be fine.

MRS. PHILLIPS

This is a needless and irresponsible risk.

PHILLIPS

This is the only way to keep meet up.

MRS. PHILLIPS

Why can't you reschedule?

PHILLIPS

Any change will affect my schedule.

MRS. PHILLIPS

Why do you always reject my counsel?

PHILLIPS

You know that is not true.

MRS. PHILLIPS

Have you sent the money to my parents?

PHILLIPS

Once I return....

MRS. PHILLIPS

Please, spare me that crap.

[She storms into the house. Phillips stares for a while, shakes his head and continues to the gate.]

MOVEMENT THREE

EXT. PHILLIPS BY THE ROADSIDE:
HAILS A TAXI. - DAY

CAST:

DRIVER

PHILLIPS

DRIVER

 Good evening and where to sir?

PHILLIPS

Abuja park please.

DRIVER

Please hop in sir.

[Phillips enters and Driver takes off.]

MOVEMENT FOUR

EXT. ABUJA PARK: TWO TOUTS
APPROACH PHILLIPS. -DAY

 CAST:

TWO TOUTS

FOURTEEN PASSENGERS

CHAIRMAN

SIENA DRIVER

FIRST TOUT

Are you heading to Abuja sir?

PHILLIPS

What type of vehicle do you have?

SECOND TOUT

His Siena is old: ours is the latest model!

FIRST TOUT

He has no passengers at all!

SECOND TOUT

We carry six and have three already!

FIRST TOUT

I need only one passenger sir.

[Phillips hands his bag to Second Tout.]

SECOND TOUT

Please follow me sir.

[Phillips follows First Tout shouts.]

FIRST TOUT

Boss, you have entered "One Chance"!

SECOND TOUT

Boss, please do not listen to that liar.

[They reach and Phillips' bag is loaded.]

PHILLIPS

How much is the fare?

SECOND TOUT

Seven thousand naira only!

[Phillips pays and the tout points him to a seat behind the driver.]

PHILLIPS

Can't I sit with the driver in front?

SECOND TOUT

Sorry sir, a passenger is already there.

PHILLIPS

Can I get a better seat than this?

SECOND TOUT

I swear that only three seats are left!

PHILLIPS

I needed leg room for the long journey.

SECOND TOUT

The driver will stop from time to time so people can eat and stretch their legs.

[Three persons arrive; Tout takes fares.]

PHILLIPS

Why collect money from all three?

SECOND TOUT

What do you mean?

PHILLIPS

You said this car takes only six!

SECOND TOUT

Boss, did anybody take your seat?

PHILLIPS

But..

SECOND TOUT

Boss, please maintain.

[One newcomer takes the front seat.]

PHILLIPS

But you told me that seat was taken?

SECOND TOUT

He just paid five hundred naira extra!

PHILLIPS

Why did you not ask me to pay extra?

SECOND TOUT

I have been working here since 1980 sir.

PHILLIPS

Meaning?

SECOND TOUT

Once I see a person, I know whether he
is a man of grammar or a man of money.

PHILLIPS

And which of the two am I?

[The driver returns with another man.]

DRIVER

Imagine the nonsense!

SECOND TOUT

What nonsense?

CHAIRMAN

Please, passengers come down.

DRIVER

Please, do not come down.

CHAIRMAN

This motor is going nowhere now.

DRIVER

Please do not come down.

PASSENGER ONE

What is the meaning of all this?

CHAIRMAN

It is not the turn of this driver.

PASSENGER TWO

So you have turned this into a habit?

DRIVER

What do you mean?

SECOND TOUT

Which people are you talking about?

PASSENGER TWO

God will punish all of you.

SECOND TOUT

All your family will die in punishment!

PHILLIPS

Calm down please.

PASSENGER TWO

I won't calm down.

PHILLIPS

There is always room for dialogue.

PASSENGER TWO

This is exactly what they did last week!

SECOND TOUT

Liar!

PASSENGER TWO

Next they will bring an old vehicle.

[Presently an older car drives close.]

CHAIRMAN

In this park, we load turn by turn: which ever turn you meet is the will of God!

PASSENGER ONE

God will surely punish you people.

SECOND TOUT

Please we can't disobey our chairman.

[All passengers but Phillips come down.]

PHILLIPS

Can you refund my money?

CHAIRMAN

In this park, there is no refund.

PHILLIPS

Okay, can I wait for the next turn?

SECOND TOUT

Boss, come down or I carry you down?

PHILLIPS

I prefer that you carry me down.

SECOND TOUT

May the gods kill you!

PHILIPS

I am waiting for you to carry me down.

SECOND TOUT

Those to kill you are waiting in Abuja!

CHAIRMAN

Sir, will you wait till next turn?

PHILLIPS

I don't mind.

[Ten minutes later others return.}

CHAIRMAN

Driver move away let another load!

[Driver comes in and starts the car.]

PASSENGER TWO

Thank you sir! If not for you...

PASSENGER ONE

I used to hear of such but now I see it!

DRIVER

Two others would have loaded while
they use my new car to lure passengers.

PASSENGER TWO

You talk as if you are not part of them.

PASSENGER ONE

Look at him trying to pull himself out.

DRIVER

They order us as they wish, if you differ
you won't enter the park again!

SECOND TOUT

[Peeps through a car window]

I think all of you are happy now?

[Passengers abuse him.]

All but one of you shall go and return!

[More passengers abuse the tout.]

Boss man, you shall go but not return!

[They depart as all abuse the tout.}

MOVEMENT FIVE

EXT. EARLY DAWN ON THE ROAD: SUDDENLY, DRIVERS ARE MAKING A U-TURN. PHILLIPS' SIENA STOPS! – MORNING.

CAST:

DRIVER AND PASSENGERS

SOLDIERS

PASSENGER ONE

Driver what is happening?

DRIVER

I see a lot of vehicles making u-turn.

PASSENGER TWO

How can when we are so close to Abuja?

[Driver waves another down.]

SIENA DRIVER

Please what is happening?

CAR DRIVER

Armed robbers have blocked the road.

[Car driver moves on. Next Siena Driver
stops a Haiku bus driver.

SIENA DRIVER

What is happening?

HAIKU DRIVER

Turn quickly: Kidnappers are operating!

[Informant dashes away. Siena Driver
stops a salon car.]

SALON DRIVER

Boko Haram has blocked the road!

[At that moment, they hear gunshots
and as the driver tries to turn, he is

blocked front and back. Many other vehicles and passengers are in disarray. Phillips watches as people run into the bush. He takes cover under the Siena.]

MOVEMENT SIX

EXT. AFTER TWO HOURS: A POLICE SIREN BLASTS FOR THREE TO FIVE MINUTES. - DAY

 CAST:

Police

Siena Driver

Phillips

Fourteen passengers

VOICE

This is the police! Come out from the bush and continue your journey. We have cleared the road.

[People wait for twenty minutes before coming despite repeated calls.]

VOICE

Put your hand as you come out!

[Five minutes more, some cars begin to warm up and more people come out.]

VOICE

As you come out, stand beside your vehicle. Only drivers sit in their car.

[Phillips comes out and stands by his Siena car. Others join him.]

VOICE

Passengers bring out your tickets and drivers bring out your manifest.

PASSENGER ONE

They did not give us a receipt oh!

PASSENGER TWO

That's true oh!

PASSENGER ONE

Even "manifest" they did not give us.

SIENA DRIVER

Keep quiet; they may not even ask you.

[As an officer approaches sporadic
gunshots ring out followed by loud
sirens. All police men double back to
their vehicles and speed off. Passengers
lie on the ground. After ten minutes,
vehicles start moving from the Abuja
end. Siena Driver waves one down.]

SIENA DRIVER

What is happening please?

ABUJA DRIVER

Police killed four of the kidnappers!

SIENA DRIVER

So the road is clear?

ABUJA DRIVER

If the road is not clear, will I be here?

SIENA DRIVER

Please get inside or I leave you here.

[All passengers scramble in and they
drive safely to Abuja.]

MOVEMENT SEVEN

EXT. ABUJA PARK: PHILLIPS HAILS
A CAB. -DAY

CAST:

PHILLIPS

TAXI CAB DRIVER

TAXI CAB DRIVER

Where sir?

PHILLIPS

International Conference Center.

CAB DRIVER

A thousand five sir.

PHILLIPS

OK.

[Driver takes him there in ten minutes:
pays the driver and walks into the hall.]

MOVEMENT EIGHT

EXT. INTERNATIONAL CONFERENCE CENTER: PHILLIPS SETS DOWN HIS VALISE BY THE DOOR AND CHECKS HIS WRIST WATCH. -DAY

CAST:

CONFERENCE CHAIRMAN

PHILLIPS

PHILLIPS

One hour to the opening!

[He calls someone on his phone.}

Yes. Just arrived! Ok, I will be waiting.

[Conference Chairman drives in later.]

CONFERENCE CHAIRMAN

Good to see you sir.

[They embrace.]

PHILLIPS

Good to see you too!

CONFERENCE CHAIRMAN

We waited throughout yesterday!

PHILLIPS

I missed my flight, so I ran at night.

CONFERENCE CHAIRMAN

Thanks for the sacrifice sir.

PHILLIPS

Do not mention sir.

CONFERENCE CHAIRMAN

Please let me take you to the hotel wing.

PHILLIPS

Do we still have the time?

CONFERENCE SPEAKER

You need to freshen up and rest!

PHILLIPS

If you insist!

[Conference Chairman picks up his bag and they enter Chairman's car and drive to the hotel wing of the complex.]

MOVEMENT NINE

EXT. CONFERENCE HALL. -DAY

CAST:

CHAIRMAN

DR. PHILLIPS

SOME CONFERENCE ATTENDEES

CHAIRMAN

On behalf *of us all, I* thank our speaker.

ALL

Yes oh!

CHAIRMAN

Please give him more applause!

ALL

Yes oh [They clap vigorously]

CHAIRMAN

It is not easy to stand up all day talking!

ANONYMOUS

Not at all Sir!

CHAIRMAN

Let alone for five days at a stretch!

ANONYMOUS

It is not easy Sir.

CHAIRMAN

May we now release him so that he can prepare for his journey tomorrow?

ANONYMOUS

Yes oh and Lagos is very far! [All rise]

CHAIRMAN

Our Father in Heaven, we thank you for your servant Dr. Phillips whom you have used for us. Please take him home safely and reward him beyond explanation!

ALL

Amen!

[They shake hands with Dr. Phillips till the last set leaves the hall with him.]

MOVEMENT TEN

EXT. BUS PARKED BY ROAD SIDE:
ALMOST FULL. DR. PHILLIPS
APPROACHES. -MORNING

CAST:

Madam

Driver

Conductor

Sergeant

Corporal

Dr. Phillips

Youth Copper One

Youth Copper Two

Female Passenger

Other passengers.

Some Police men

CONDUCTOR

Are you going to Lagos Sir?

PHILLIPS

Yes please!

CONDUCTOR

You are very lucky Sir!

PHILLIPS

How?

CONDUCTOR

We have only one sit left Sir!

PHILLIPS

Are you sure?

CONDUCTOR

I swear with my grandmother.

PHILLIPS

Please, you do not need to swear.

CONDUCTOR

Sincerely Sir, you are the last passenger.

[Dr. hands in his bag and they issue him with a receipt and ask him to take a seat. Then a man gets down.]

PHILLIPS

Vendor!

VENDOR

Sir!

[Rushes to Dr. Phillips}

PHILLIPS

Give me "Punch" and two other papers."

VENDOR

Yes Sir.

[Dr. Phillip pays and starts reading.]

CONDUCTOR

Thank God, the last passenger has come.

YOUTH CORPER ONE

What are you talking about?

CONDUCTOR

Copper, please allow me to do my work.

DRIVER

Please load the motor: let me leave here or what concerns you with the Copper?

CONDUCTOR

Madam, bring your money.

MADAM

I cannot pay without seeing my seat!

DRIVER

Newspaper man, can you please go
down and allow Madam to come inside?

PHILLIPS

Why not?

[Phillips begins to step down.]

MADAM

Why are you going down?

PHILLIPS

A woman should not sit by the door.

MADAM

So I should go inside?

PHILLIPS

That is why I came down for you.

MADAM

So this is you people's plan?

DRIVER

Madam, come inside in case the door opens by accident!

MADAM

Your evil plan will not work?

DRIVER

I am only trying to protect you.

MADAM

Shut up, you evil man.

[Woman steps down.]

YOUTH CORPER TWO

Madam, please we are all traveling.

MADAM

You even do kidnapping with uniform!

YOUTH CORPER TWO

We are genuine coppers Ma.

MADAM

[LAUGHS]

 Conductor, refund my money before I count three!

PHILLIPS

Madam, look at me!

MADAM

Yes, why should I look at you.

PHILLIPS

I am too old for the kind of thing.

MADAM

Even people older than you are doing it!

CONDUCTOR

Madam, go in and let the driver move!

MADAM

Instead of me to enter let trailer jam me!

FEMALE PASSENGER

Driver refund her money please!

YOUTH COPPER ONE

Yes, she is causing a scene.

CONDUCTOR

Money paid cannot be refunded.

[Crowd begins to build up as the woman raises her voice while Conductor remains adamant. Police Patrol arrives.]

SERGEANT

What is going on here?

MADAM

They are kidnappers and ritual killers!

DRIVER

Your family members are kidnappers!

MADAM

Thief!

CONDUCTOR

Watch it or I deal with you here now.

SERGEANT

Stop that: are you fighting a woman?

MADAM

Did I not tell you they are criminals?

[Conductor slaps woman. She falls in a faint and they rush her to hospital while Conductor and Driver are arrested. The two youth-coppers take their loads out of the bus but they are stopped.]

SERGEANT

For now, you are not under arrest but pray that the woman does not die.

YOUTH COPPER ONE

God will not let her die.

YOUTH COPPER TWO

Did the Sergeant not see who hit her?

FEMALE PASSENGER

The woman is imitating senators!

YOUTH COPPER ONE

You mean the woman is acting?

FEMALE PASSENGER

Please do not quote me oh!

SERGEANT

You all must come to the station!

YOUTH COPPER TWO

What is bringing that one?

SERGEANT

You happen to be in this vehicle.

YOUTH COPPER ONE

A vehicle that could not fill up since!

SERGEANT

Please, all of you: follow me to the station so that we take your statements on time and you can proceed on your journey.]

[THEY ALL FOLLOW HIM]

MOVEMENT ELEVEN

EXT. AT THE ABUJA POLICE
STATION. –DAY.

CAST

Sergeant

Corporal

Dr. Phillips

Youth Copper One

Youth Copper Two

Female Passenger

Other passengers

Some Police men

PHILLIPS

Can I have a word with you Sergeant?

SERGEANT

Take the rest inside.

[Goes aside with Dr. Phillips]

PHILLIPS

Can I see your privately sir?

SERGEANT

There is An allegation of attempted
kidnapping against all of you.

CORPER ONE

You mean you believe that woman?

SERGEANT

What I believe is irrelevant.

CORPER ONE

How?

SERGEANT

My job is to investigate: not opinionate.

PHILLIPS

That is why I and others followed you.

SERGEANT

So what do you want me to do?

PHILLIPS

I want a private word with you please.

SERGEANT

May I know you Sir?

[They step aside while a corporal takes others into the station.]

PHILLIPS

This is my identity card.

[Hands him a card and he takes a look.]

SERGEANT

You should have shown me this since.

PHILLIPS

What can you arrange?

SERGEANT

I will get a car to drop you in Lagos Sir!

[Presently, a corporal runs to Sergeant]

CORPORAL

Sir, the woman is dead!

SERGEANT

What?

CORPORAL

She died on arrival.

SERGEANT

Have you locked all the people up?

CORPORAL

I did before rushing to inform you.

SERGEANT

Go and make sure.

[Corporal hurries away]

PHILLIPS

What advice do you have?

SERGEANT

It was a fight between those two that
fought: I will find you another vehicle.
PHILLIPS

Ok. I really appreciate it.

[They exit.]

MOVEMENT TWELVE

EXT. MAIN ROAD TO LAGOS. –DAY.

[Sergeant stops two cars who apologize for not being able to reach Lagos. A three-car convoy stops. Sergeant waves the lead car down.]

CAST:

Sergeant

Phillips

Denis

Woman

Two other drivers

DENIS

Sergio!

SERGEANT

Ah, is this not Denis?

DENIS

Sergio, it is me.

[They shake hands]

SERGEANT

Why are you leaving so late?

DENIS

Our cars arrived late and we still have to deliver to Lagos before 8am tomorrow.

SERGEANT

Please drop this boss in Lagos.

DENIS

You know him well?

SERGEANT

Yes.

DENIS

Sir, please get inside.

PHILLIPS

Oh! That's great. Thanks.

[As he gets in a woman comes to beg.]

WOMAN

Please driver, help me: I am going to Lagos and no motor as you can see.

DENIS

This is not a commercial vehicle.

WOMAN

But you can help me Sir.

SERGEANT

Do you have anything to identify you?

WOMAN

Yes, here is my identity card.

[Sergeant takes a look.]

SERGEANT

She is a nurse with the teaching hospital.

DENIS

It is illegal for us to carry passengers.

SERGEANT

This can be an exception.

DENIS

Get inside please.

[She thanks him and gets inside.]

SERGEANT

Thank you Denis!

DENIS

I will visit the barracks when I return.

SERGEANT

No problem! Journey mercies Sir.

PHILLIPS

Thanks so much, Sergeant.

[As they drive off, Sergeant walks away.]

MOVEMENT THIRTEEN

EXT. TWO HOURS LATER: CUSTOMS CHECKPOINT. -DAY

CAST:

Two Custom Officers

Customs Inspector

Denis

Dr. Phillips

Nurse

Two other drivers

CUSTOM OFFICER

Two of your vehicles are under invoiced.

DENIS

That is certainly not true.

CUSTOMS OFFICER

That is what everyone says.

DENIS

We deal on cars and deliver regularly.

CUSTOMS OFFICER

We collect revenue regularly.

DENIS

We paid the duty we were asked to pay.

CUSTOMS OFFICER

Our check indicates under invoicing.

DENIS

You are delaying me unnecessarily.

CUSTOMS OFFICER

Pay the difference or we tow the car!

DENIS

It is not my duty to pay custom duties.

NURSE

Please officer, show some mercy.

CUSTOMS OFFICER

I will put you in another vehicle.

DENIS

Both of you can follow his alternative.

PHILLIPS

We can wait while you settle this.

DENIS

No Sir. I know both of you are in haste.

NURSE

But we can still beg the officers.

DENIS

Just go: the officer is inconsiderate.

PHILLIPS

Are you sure we should leave you?

DENIS

We are used to this type of thing.

PHILLIPS

I am truly sorry.

DENIS

No problem.

[The Custom Officer flags a bus and talks to the driver who picks up the NURSE and Dr. Phillips]

MOVEMENT FOURTEEN

EXT. AFTER THREE MORE HOURS:
POLICE CHECKPOINT. DRIVER HITS
POLICE MAN. POLICE SURROUND
THE VEHICLE. - DAY

CAST:

SEVERAL POLICE MEN

DRIVER AND PASSENGERS

INSPECTOR

Come down before count three!

ANONYMOUS POLICE

Put your hands up as you come out!

[All come down.]

INSPECTOR

Search them one by one!

[Driver rushes to help accident victim.]

INSPECTOR

Where is the driver?

DRIVER

I am here sir!

INSPECTOR

Where?

DRIVER

I am attending to the injured man sir.

INSPECTOR

You want to add to his injuries?

DRIVER

No sir.

INSPECTOR

Okoro, arrest the man immediately.

OKORO

Yes sir.

DRIVER

I am a policeman sir.

INSPECTOR

Is Police running commercial service?

DRIVER

I am off duty sir.

INSPECTOR

Is that a license to drive recklessly?

DRIVER

No sir.

INSPECTOR

Let me see your ID card.

DRIVER

Here it is sir!

[Inspector inspects the card.]

INSPECTOR

This is an expired card!

DRIVER

I used my pension to buy this bus.

INSPECTOR

You are even wearing a police cap?

DRIVER

Sorry sir.

INSPECTOR

Do the police owe you?

DRIVER

No sir.

INSPECTOR

Then who sent you to kill us?

DRIVER

The brake failed sir.

INSPECTOR

You and your co-travelers are suspects.

DRIVER

 It was a brake failure.

[Oncoming vehicle shines light on them.
Injured man recognizes the Driver]

CORPORAL BEN

Is that you Pat?

DRIVER

The Devil is a liar!

CORPORAL BEN

Sir, this man is my blood brother!

DRIVER

Imagine! My own brother!

[Both men speak vernacular.]

INSPECTOR

Take Lance Corporal Ben to the hospital immediately for I can see that the accident has affected his brain.

CORPORAL BEN

I am ok sir.

INSPECTOR

You see what I am saying?

OKORO

No sir.

INSPECTOR

Can a speeding vehicle hit somebody and he will still be alright?

BEN

Sir, I jumped away on time.

OKORO

But I saw you thrown up, with my eyes?

BEN

I dived for safety: he only hit my torch.

INSPECTOR

Can you see the non-sense he is saying?

OKORO

He looks normal anyway.

INSPECTOR

Take him to the hospital now!

DRIVER

Please Inspector, I meant no harm.

INSPECTOR

I can only be sure after a medical report.

[Okoro leads the injured man away.]

INSPECTOR

Now search the vehicle thoroughly!

[Two search and find a vehicle engine]

CONSTABLE

We suspect this engine sir.

INSPECTOR

Who is the owner of this motor engine?

TRADER

I am the one and I have the receipt.

INSPECTOR

Constable, take all here to the station!

DRIVER

Please, we are still going to Lagos.

INSPECTOR

What if you had died in the accident?

DRIVER

Please officer: reconsider.

TRADER

Please sir, we are sorry.

INSPECTOR

Your own case is worse because you
have to show us who issued you that
receipt and he will in turn, show us the
one with which he imported the engine!

CONSTABLE

Everybody, get into the bus!

DRIVER

Please sir: help me beg the Inspector.

PHILLIPS

Officer please, can I see you privately?

[He moves towards the officer]

INSPECTOR

Why are you following me?

PHILLIPS

Can I have a private word with you?

INSPECTOR

Go to the station and state your case.

PHILLIPS

I want to tell you something secret.

INSPECTOR

Go to the point sir.

[Phillips whispers something to him.]

INSPECTOR

Constable!

CONSTABLE

Sir!

INSPECTOR

Come down from the bus!

CONSTABLE

Yes sir!

INSPECTOR

I take them while you remain here!

CONSTABLE

Yes sir!

INSPECTOR

[Inspector gets in with others.]

Driver, hope you know Div Two HQ?

DRIVER

Yes sir.

INSPECTOR

Then drive straight there.

[The driver drives away.]

MOVEMENT FIFTEEN

EXT. DIVISION TWO HQ: BUS PARKS
IN FRONT. -DAY

CAST: Same cast as in Movement
Fourteen]

INSPECTOR

Wait here please.

[Goes and returns with the injured Ben.
Driver embraces Ben.]

DRIVER

God I thank you for keeping my brother.

BEN

Please drive more carefully.

DRIVER

I will. Inspector thanks please.

INSPECTOR

Thank both God and the Boss in front.

DRIVER

I thank all of you sir.

[Others join in thanking the Inspector.]

INSPECTOR

Please leave before I change my mind.

[Driver drives off.]

MOVEMENT SIXTEEN

INT. THE PHILLIPS' HOME. -DAY

CAST:

MRS. PHILLIPS

KATE

DOCTOR

ROSE

MRS. PHILLIPS

Kate!

KATE

Yes Madam.

MRS. PHILLIPS

I have not seen Rose this morning!

KATE

She was sleeping when I visited last.

MRS. PHILLIPS

And she is still sleeping up to now?

KATE

I think so ma!

MRS. PHILLIPS

 Go and wake her up for school!

[Rose goes in and returns.]

KATE

Ma, Rose is not waking up!

MRS. PHILLIPS

What? Go and carry her here.

[Kate goes and returns with Rose who fails to respond to all efforts to wake her up. Mrs. Phillips calls a doctor who examines her.]

DOCTOR

She died in her sleep!

[Mrs. Phillips faints.]

MOVEMENT SEVENTEEN

EXT. A MILITARY CHECKPOINT:
SOLDIER LOOKS INTO THE BUS.
IDENTIFIES TWO YOUTHS! –DAY.

CAST;

PASSENGERS

DRIVER

PHILLIPS

SOLDIER

You and you come down.

[The identified persons come down.]

SOLDIER

Identify yourselves.

STUDENT

I am a student of John Polytechnic sir.

SOLDIER

Bring out your identity card.

STUDENT

I forgot my ID card at home.

SOLDIER

Do you know you look like a criminal?

STUDENT

This is Bob Marley hairstyle sir.

SOLDIER

A lot of criminals wear this hair style.

STUDENT

I am a student sir.

SOLDIER

You see those people sitting over there?

[Points]

STUDENT

Yes sir.

SOLDIER

Go there and sit down.

[The student goes.]

SOLDIER

Yes you, are you a soldier?

MUSICIAN

No, I am a musician.

SOLDIER

Why are you to wearing camouflage?

MUSICIAN

This is not camouflage sir.

SOLDIER

Are you to teach me what camouflage is?

MUSICIAN

No sir.

SOLDIER

Go there and sit with those suspects.

MUSICIAN

I have a show to meet up in Lagos!

SOLDIER

And common sense did not tell you that even if you are going to play the part of a soldier in a play, you wait until you get to the dressing room before wearing the soldier's uniform?

MUSICIAN

Sorry sir but...

SOLDIER

Go sit with others or I double you up.

[Musician goes over while the soldier moves off. They wait for ten minutes.]

PASSENGER ONE

Driver, go and ask the soldier if we should go. We cannot just keep waiting.

DRIVER

Do you think the man forgot us?

PASSENGER TWO

Other vehicles are moving past.

DRIVER

Let us wait.

[Just then, the soldier comes to them.]

SOLDIER

Driver, go with these people.

DRIVER

Thank you sir!

[Driver starts the car.]

PASSENGER ONE

Officer, what of our other passengers?

SOLDIER

Which one is your brother?

PASSENGER ONE

None!

SOLDIER

One must be your partner in crime?

PASSENGER ONE

None!

SOLDIER

Come down now or I drag you down!

PASSENGER ONE

Why should I come down?

SOLDIER

We are also arresting suspected accomplices!

PASSENGER ONE

I am a Building Engineer and I have my identification papers to prove who I am.

SOLDIER

Even ***Boko Haram*** has those papers.

PASSENGER ONE

Well, I am not ***Boko Haram.***

SOLDIER

Alright, come and show me the papers.

[Passenger One climbs obeys. Soldier peers into the documents.]

SOLDIER

The light is so bad, I cannot read.

PASSENGER ONE

Driver, lend us your torchlight.

SOLDIER

Officer!

SERGEANT

Yes?

SOLDIER

Sir please, let people in the tent help me look for my reading glass. I have some papers to read here.

SERGEANT

Where did you keep it?

SOLDIER

On the table!

SERGEANT

Ok, they will start looking for it.

SOLDIER

While they are looking for my eye-glass,
go and sit with those people.

PASSENGER ONE

What?

SOLDIER

Move before I move you!

PHILLIPS

Engineer: do as he says!

[Engineer crosses to join others.]

PHILLIPS

Officer, permit me to come down.

SOLDIER

Do you want to urinate?

PHILLIPS

Permit me to have a word with you.

SOLDIER

Is it about the people sitting over there?

PHILLIPS

I have secret information.

SOLDIER

Okay sir.

[Phillips and Soldier move away, whisper and return.]

SOLDIER

Three of you, come here!

[The three come over.]

PHILLIPS

How can you be travel at night without any identification? And you why camouflage? Apologize for your offense.

STUDENT

I am sorry sir.

MUSICIAN

Can I throw it away here?

SOLDIER

Change into a civilian dress and hand
the camouflage to me. Otherwise, if you
get to another checkpoint and the dress
is found, that would be more trouble!

[They all thank the Soldier: Musician
hands him the camouflage, changes into
shirt from his bag and Driver zooms off.]

MOVEMENT EIGHTEEN

EXT. TWO HOURS LATER. LAGOS LONG BRIDGE: HEAVY GO-SLOW.- DAY.

 CAST:

Nurse

Student

Phillips

Taxi Driver

Four Robbers

Passengers

NURSE

This is terrible!

STUDENT

After all the stress, imagine this go-slow.

NURSE

I cannot meet up my shift.

DRIVER

Thank God that this one is moving.

[Just then, four boys armed with rods approach: two from the front and two from the rear. One of the rear boys shatters the boot's glass with a heavy rod while the other hits the body of the van with his own noise. As the occupants turn in shock to the rear, the first of the two boys coming from the front pokes his hand into the vehicle and snatches Nurse's bags while the other one slaps Phillips squarely on his face. The other one dips his hand into Phillips' breast pocket and collects whatever he could find while the one that slapped him before, hit him on the chest with his rod.]

FIRST REAR ROBBER

Shut up or you die!

[Everyone is quiet. The Second Rear
Robber produces a bag from nowhere.
People in other vehicles are seen exiting
and running helter-skelter.]

SECOND REAR ROBBER

Drop your money, phones, laptops, ATM
card here quickly. If I search you and
find anything, you are dead!

FIRST REAR ROBBER

Now!

[Occupants empty their bags and
pockets into the robbers' bag and the
robbers jump into neighboring bushes.
Suddenly, the road is clear and other
drivers are driving speedily away.]

ANONYMOUS DRIVER

Driver, get inside and move or those
boys will come back and meet you!

[Phillips driver enters and drives away
while Phillips is clutching his chest
where the robber hit him with the rod
and the Nurse is assisting him.]

MOVEMENT NINETEEN

EXT. BERGER BUS STOP: DRIVER PARKS. –DAY.

CAST:

Bus Driver

Passengers

Phillips

Nurse

DRIVER

This is my last bus stop.

PASSENGER ONE

Did you not say you will get to Ojota?

DRIVER

I did but the situation has changed.

PASSENGER ONE

How?

DRIVER

The law requires me to report this robbery to the nearest police station to the crime scene. Moreover, the owner of the vehicle will not believe unless I have a police report.

[All passengers come down and pick their loads. Phillips is seen showing signs of great pains. A crowd builds up asking driver questions. Nurse helps Phillips pick up his valise and head towards the car park.]

MOVEMENT TWENTY

EXT. FRONT THE TAXI PARK.-
EVENING.

CAST:

Nurse

Phillips

Taxi Driver

NURSE

I think you should go straight to hospital. Sir, are you hearing me? Sir, are you okay?

[Phillips nods.]

NURSE

Taxi: take us to the nearest hospital.

PHILLIPS

Number 10 Bello Street, Yaba.

NURSE

What?

PHILLIPS

Number 10 Bello Street, Yaba

TAXI DRIVER

Number 10 Bello Street, Yaba.

[Driver opens the back seat for them and zooms off through the streets.]

MOVEMENT TWENTY-ONE

EXT. NUMBER 10 BELLO STREET, YABA.- EVENING.

[Nurse helps Phillips to the front and they press the button. No response. So Phillips tries to bang on the door but too feeble. Taxi Driver helps bang louder.]

CAST:

Mrs. Phillips

Phillips

Nurse

Taxi Driver

MRS. PHILLIPS

Who is that?

NURSE

Your husband!

MRS. PHILLIPS

Can't he speak for himself?

NURSE

Please open the door Ma!

MRS. PHILLIPS

I can't open till I hear my husband's voice.

TAXI DRIVER

[Comes forward and bangs heavily. Madam fires: a bullet hits the Taxi Driver who falls. Phillips also falls to the ground. The door is wide open enabling Mrs. Phillips to see the Nurse and the two men on the floor.]

MRS. PHILLIPS

And who may you be?

NURSE

I....I...Traveled with him from Abuja.

MRS. PHILLIPS

You are the reason he didn't answer my
calls?

NURSE

No! No! No!

MRS. PHILLIPS

What an insult!

[Mrs. Phillips shoots the Nurse and
walks back into the main house. Phillips
gets up and staggers blindly away.
Under ten minutes, police arrive.]

MOVEMENT TWENTY-TWO

EXT. THIRD MAINLAND BRIDGE. –
EVENING.

Phillips is seen staggering on the road with his hand still clutching his chest. A female driver goes past. Then stops and reverses while others are speeding past. She fires the reversed vehicle towards the staggering man and drives dangerously between him and the bridge culvert. She knocks him down somehow and other drivers begin to stop. A police patrol car arrives immediately.

CAST:

Police Officers

Pastor

Female Driver

Phillips

FEMALE DRIVER

I believed he was about to jump into the
lagoon.

PASTOR

From the other side of the road
staggering dangerously!

POLICE OFFICER

Please give him space to get fresh air.
We want to record the scene quickly and
rushing him to Island General Hospital.

[People give space as police take
pictures and later take Phillips to
hospital. The Female driver and the
Pastor follow. Others remain talking
about the incident.]

MOVEMENT TWENTY-THREE

EXT. A WEEK LATER: NUMBER 10 BELLOW STREET. - DAY

[Chief Koko, and two other chiefs are in front. Two Police men stand guard.]

CAST:

THREE CHIEFS

TWO CONSTABLES

OLD WOMAN

CHIEF DIDI

Officer, we want to see our brother.

1ST CONSTABLE

Who is your brother?

CHIEF DIDI

The owner of the house!

2ND CONSTABLE

What do you want with him?

CHIEF KOKO

He promised us something this week.

1ST CONSTABLE

If you do not go away, I will shoot you.

CHIEF DIDI

Go ahead and shoot us idiot.

[1st Constable cocks his gun but the other one stops him.]

2ND CONSTABLE

It is trespassers they say we should shoot: not busy-body people.

[The old woman appears.]

OLD WOMAN

I have been visiting for three days and this two say I have lost my bubbles.

CHIEF KOKO

Who are you?

OLD WOMAN

I have come to collect like you people.

CHIEF DIDI

What are you collecting?

OLD WOMAN

The thing Abuja people collect with big bags but give us with tablespoon.

1ST CONSTABLE

Thank God, I now understand.

2ND CONSTABLE

What do you understand?

1ST CONSTABLE

These are the people who made the Boss
to follow the night bus instead of the
aero plane to Abuja! We must arrest
them to give evidence in court.

CHIEF DIDI

Constable what did you just say?

2ND CONSTABLE

You are all under arrest for helping
Abuja people steal our money.

CHIEF KOKO

God forbid. Since they gave birth to me,
I have never seen a person who resides
in Abuja!

CHIEF DIDI

Please where is the road to Yaba
Polytechnic: that's where I am going.

CHIEF JAMES

We only stopped to ask you the road.

OLD WOMAN

As for me, I am going to Yaba market.

1ST CONSTABLE

Okay follow straight and keep going: never look back till you count ten thousand!

ALL

Thank you sirs!

[And they hurry away.]

1ST CONSTABLE

You see how they push politicians into theft.

2ND CONSTABLE

Please come let us play our game: they have no shame!

[They resume their seat.]

MOVEMENT TWENTY-FOUR

INT. TWO WEEKS LATER. YABA
HIGH COURT. – DAY.

[The court is sitting.]

REGISTRAR

The next case is Lagos State versus Mrs.
Phillips in a matter of attempted murder
and aggravated bodily harm. Is Mrs.
Phillips in court?

MRS. PHILLIPS

Yes please.

REGISTRAR

Please step forward.

[She does and the Registrar administers the oath.]

JUDGE

What is your plea Mrs. Phillips?

MRS. PHILLIPS

Not guilty, please.

JUDGE

The Prosecutor may now proceed.

STATE ATTORNEY GENERAL

 [Steps forward.]

We hereby enter a ***nolle prosequi.***

[Prosecutor presents the letter to the Registrar who presents it to the judge}

JUDGE

This case is hereby struck out and the accused: discharged and acquitted.

I dare say that it is a great honor to have the Attorney General in person in his court!

ATTORNEY-GENERAL

Thanks so much Your Honor.

[Mrs. Phillips happily exits court.]

REGISTRAR

The next case is Lagos State versus Mr. Phillips in a matter of attempted suicide. Is Mr. Phillips in court?

PHILLIPS

Yes please.

[He steps into the dock and an oath is administered on him.}

JUDGE

What is your plea Mr. Phillip?

PHILLIPS

Not guilty Sir.

JUDGE

The Prosecutor may now proceed.

ATTORNEY GENERAL

We hereby enter a ***nolle prosequi.***

[He presents a paper to the Registrar who passes the same to the Judge who studies it.]

JUDGE

This case is hereby struck out: Mr. D. Phillips discharged and acquitted.

[Mr. Phillips happily exits the court.]

REGISTRAR

The next cases is a joint suit for One Billion naira in damages, from Mrs. Phillips of 10 Bello St, Yaba by Nurse Mary Young of Teaching Hospital Mushin and Mr. Yinka Salami, a registered taxi driver for bodily harm and trauma occasioned by her shooting at them on the 2nd of October. Are the plaintiffs in court?

PLAINTIFFS LAWYER

Yes, Your Honor and we apply to withdraw the case via this letter. My clients have been adequately compensated verbally and monetarily in an out-of-court settlement.

[Letter is collected and passed on.]

JUDGE

This case is hereby struck out. I shall now rise.

[The Judge leaves. Court audience co-mingles and greet happily.]

MOVEMENT TWENTY-FIVE

EXT. FRONT OF THE COURT. – DAY.

[Press men block the way as people come out of the court.]

CAST:

JOURNALIST

ATTORNEY GENERAL

NEWSSLAP

Mr. Attorney-General: why did you enter ***nolle prosequi*** in both cases?

ATTORNEY GENERAL

The Governor considered Mr. Phillips motive in taking the night bus, which help the poor. Governor also found that Phillips was not about to commit suicide but was driven and confused by extreme pain and trauma. Medical doctors also confirmed to His Excellency that such is possible in similar circumstances.

NEWSSLAP

What of the wife who shot two persons?

ATTORNEY-GENERAL

Her gun license stands withdrawn. His Excellency also considered three things:

1. She lost her only child while her husband was away.
2. He was presumed dead only for him to appear with a strange woman. Imagine her mind then.
3. Also, she came to the door to defend for the banging was unusual and not to murder.

NEWSSLAP

Rumors have it that husband and wife are top security people in the country.

ATTORNEY GENERAL

I don't listen to rumors. Good day!

[He walks away while pressmen try to
ask more questions.]

THE END

www.ingramcontent.com/pod-product-compliance
Lightning Source LLC
Chambersburg PA
CBHW051437140726
47987CB00006B/2410